A Life in Pictures
Elvis Presley

Marie Clayton

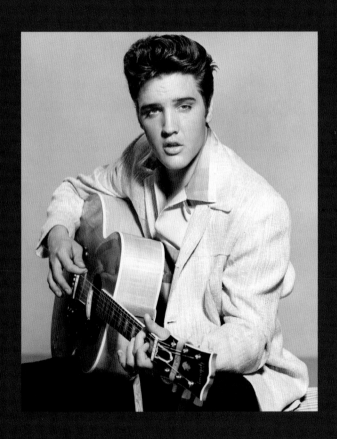

Trans
Atlantic
Press

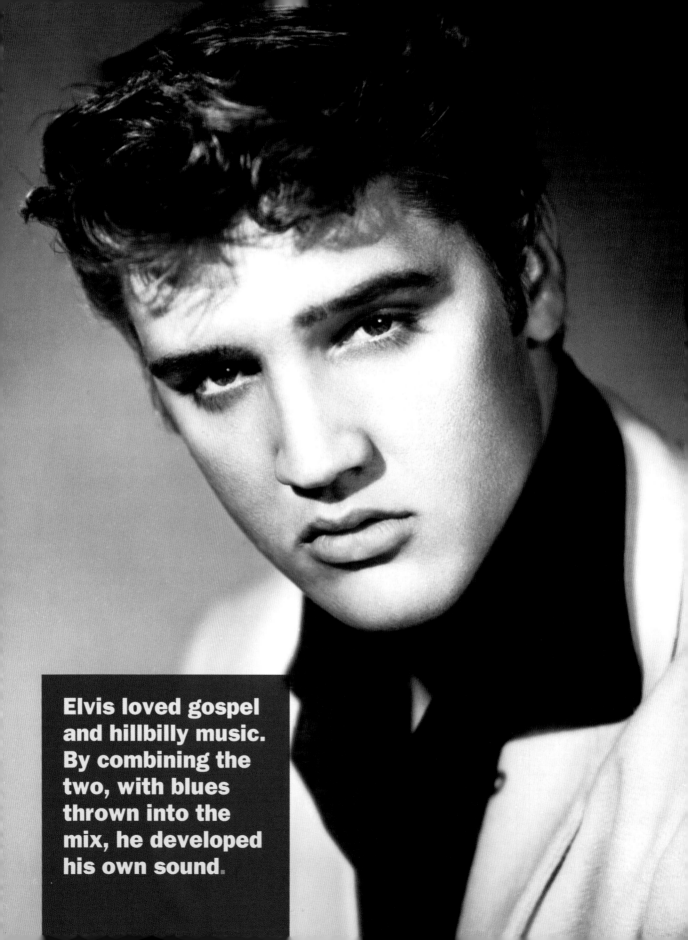

Elvis loved gospel and hillbilly music. By combining the two, with blues thrown into the mix, he developed his own sound.

A star is born

Elvis Aaron Presley was born on January 8, 1935, in Tupelo, Mississippi. Elvis grew up listening to live gospel music, as well as country and western on the radio. Since his family could not afford lessons, he taught himself to play the piano and learned the guitar from a family friend. He had a real ear for music and a very good memory, so he could play a song perfectly after hearing it just a couple of times.

In 1953 Elvis recorded a song at Sun Records in Memphis, a studio owned by Sam Phillips and Marion Keisker. Nothing came of it immediately and Elvis continued with his regular job as a truck driver. However, Sam Phillips called him back a while later and set him rehearsing with two much more experienced musicians, Scotty Moore (pictured above with Elvis) and Bill Black. The three of them recorded a blues number, "That's All Right, Mama", and soon afterwards a local disc jockey, Dewey Phillips, played the record around 14 times in one evening on his "Red Hot and Blue" show.

Success at the Louisiana Hayride

Above: Despite his new-found success as a singer, Elvis continued to drive a truck for Crown Electric during the day until Elvis and the Blue moon Boys began performing at the Louisiana Hayride, which was broadcast on KWKH from the Municipal Auditorium in Shreveport. They first appeared here on October 16, 1954, and soon signed a contract to appear weekly on a Saturday night. By the end of 1954 they were touring almost full-time. They often appeared in one venue, then drove all night to appear somewhere else, with only a few hours' sleep in the back of the car.

Opposite: Elvis was advertised as "the freshest, newest voice in country music".

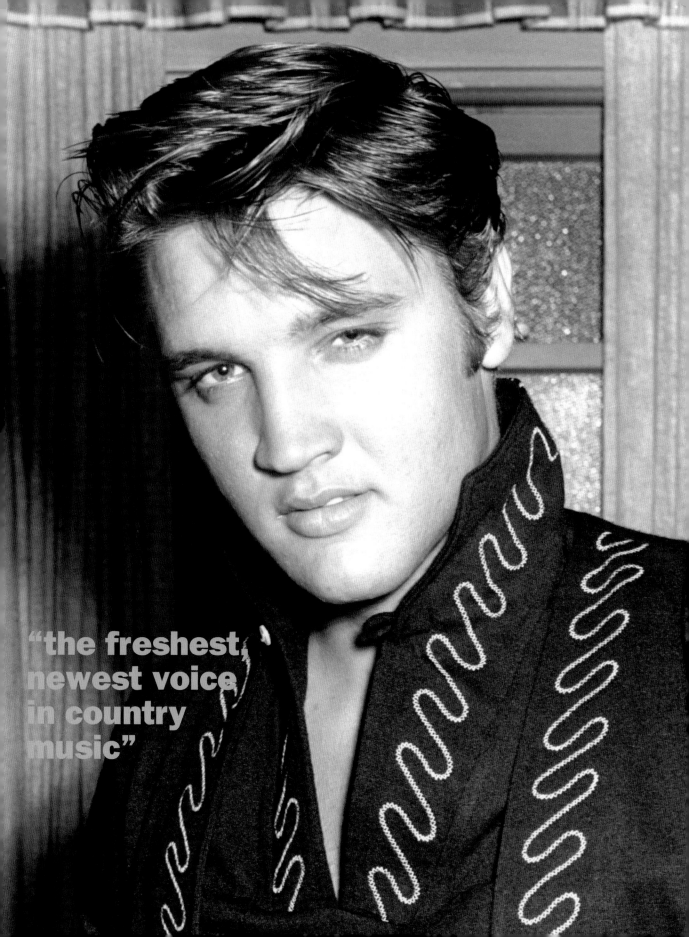

"the freshest, newest voice in country music"

Elvis released "Baby, Let's Play House"/"I'm Left, You're Right, She's Gone" in April 1955. By July the record had made it into the *Billboard* Top 10—Elvis's first appearance in the charts.

Teaming up with the Colonel

Although by the end of 1954 the boys were famous locally, mainly on the country music circuit, they had still not achieved national recognition—but it was not to be long in coming. In October 1954 they were brought to the attention of Colonel Tom Parker (above), a showbusiness promoter who was famous for his business acumen. After noticing the overheated audience reaction to Elvis, the Colonel realized he was on to something special, and soon began moves to take over. He started by getting bookings further afield.

Opposite: Female fans went wild as Elvis swivelled his hips and shook his legs—most singers of the time hardly moved as they performed.

Elvis's first album, *Elvis Presley*, was released in March 1956 and stayed on the *Billboard* chart for 68 weeks.

A change of lifestyle

Above: Elvis signs autographs for a group of young fans. Due to the demands of his career, coupled with the increasing problem of having to deal with hysterical fans whenever he went out, Elvis's movements were becoming more and more restricted. He was already at least one step removed from "normal" life, and was beginning to lay down the foundations for the lifestyle that was ultimately to lead to his downfall.

It was rumoured that at the start of Elvis's career the Colonel had paid girls to scream at his concerts—but it certainly wasn't necessary by this time, if it had ever been. As well as being an exciting and talented performer, Elvis was very handsome and knew instinctively how to charm everyone around him.

Signing with RCA

Opposite: Elvis receives his first gold record, after "Heartbreak Hotel" sells a million copies. Atlantic Records bid $25,000 for Elvis, but were turned down but in November 1955 RCA bought Elvis's contract from Sam Phillips for $35,000. Elvis himself received $5,000, which he used to buy a car. Despite the fears of RCA executives, Elvis's first single quickly proved to be a massive hit, reaching No. 1 on the *Billboard* pop chart as well as No. 1 on the *Billboard* country chart.

Above: Elvis sang his new single, "Hound Dog," for the first time on television on *The Milton Berle Show* in 1956. The audience appeared to love the song and their reaction encouraged Elvis to new heights.

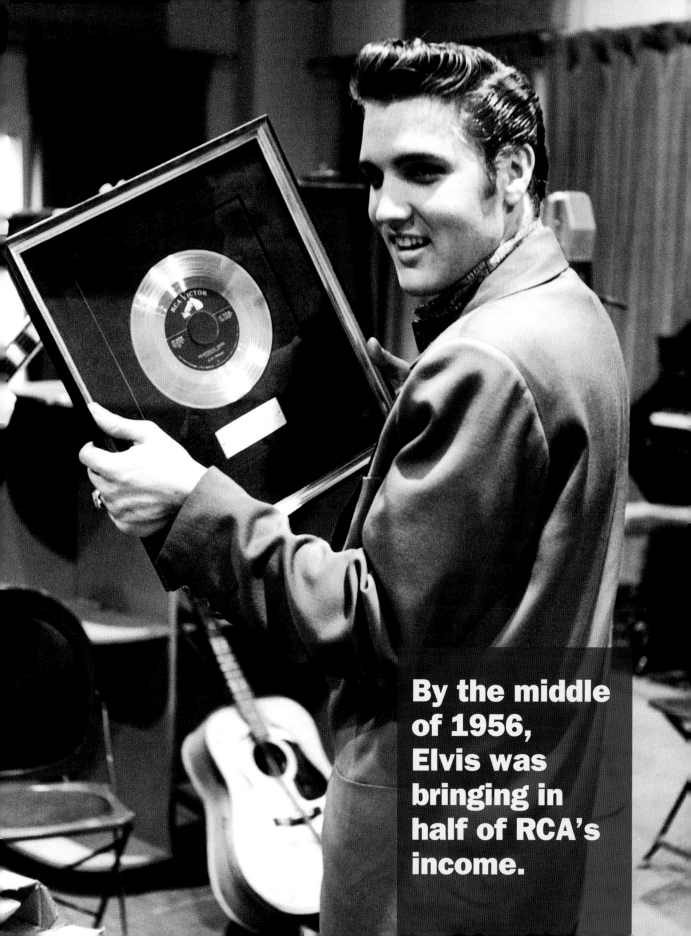

By the middle
of 1956,
Elvis was
bringing in
half of RCA's
income.

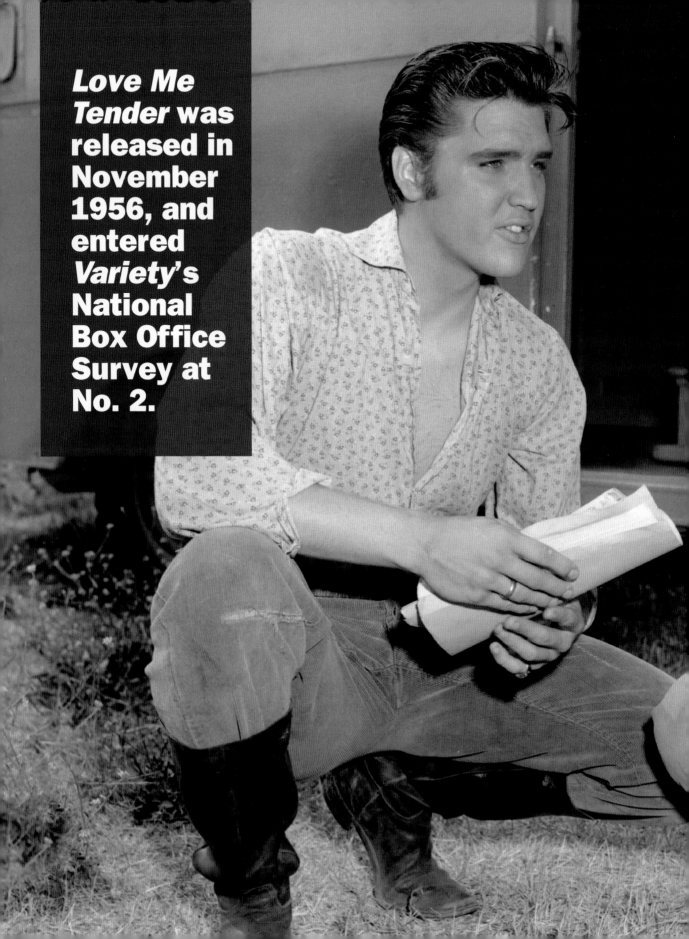

Love Me Tender was released in November 1956, and entered *Variety*'s National Box Office Survey at No. 2.

Love Me Tender

Left: Elvis on set during filming of his first movie, *Love Me Tender*, with co-star Debra Paget. Although Elvis had a three-picture contract with Paramount, they initially had no suitable vehicle for him so they loaned him out to Twentieth Century Fox for this Civil War drama. This is the only Elvis movie that was not written specifically for him, and critical reviews for his performance were rather mixed, but director David Weisbart—who had directed James Dean in *Rebel Without a Cause*—thought he had great natural ability. The movie was originally entitled *The Reno Brothers*, but after Elvis had a massive hit with one of the featured songs, "Love Me Tender", the movie title was altered to match.

Highest ratings in television history

Above: Ed Sullivan with Elvis during rehearsals for an appearance on his show. The Colonel had approached Sullivan about featuring Elvis earlier, but had been firmly turned down. However, once Sullivan saw what Elvis did to the ratings he backed down and booked him for three appearances—at a fee of $50,000, which was rather more than the Colonel had originally asked for, and triple Sullivan's previous highest fee.

Opposite: By the time Elvis appeared on *The Ed Sullivan Show* for the third time, he had earned the nickname "Elvis the Pelvis" and Sullivan had become concerned for his "family show" image. To avoid problems Sullivan decided to crop Elvis—and he was filmed only from the waist up. It has been estimated that at least one of the three Sullivan performances was seen by 52 million people: one out of every three Americans at the time.

Elvis's second appearance on *The Ed Sullivan Show* featured a performance of the song "Love Me Tender" which resulted in advance orders of two million copies.

Moving to Graceland

Above: As soon as Elvis had sufficient money he bought a new house for his parents and himself, but as he became more famous, fans began to hang around outside in their hundreds. This was not only intruding on the Presleys' lives but was also extremely annoying for their neighbours, and Elvis decided that they needed a home with more privacy. The Presleys fell in love with Graceland and Gladys was really happy to move in, planning her own chicken coop and hog pen, but she soon began to feel very isolated. Elvis was always away touring, and when he was at home she had very little time with him as Graceland had also become home to many members of his permanent entourage, as well as a floating population of acquaintances.

Opposite: Meanwhile Elvis had completed his second movie, *Loving You*, for Paramount, with Dolores Hart and Lizabeth Scott. Elvis's hair was dyed black for the part of Deke Rivers and it suited him well—he was naturally a dark blond, but he kept it black for the rest of his life.

In 1956 Elvis released two LPs, *Elvis* and *Elvis Presley*, both of which went gold, and four classic singles "Heartbreak Hotel," "Hound Dog," "Love Me Tender" and "I Want You, I Need You, I Love You".

The single "Jailhouse Rock" sold more than three million copies in one year in the US and became Elvis's first No. 1 record in the UK.

Jailhouse Rock

Opposite: A still from *Jailhouse Rock*, which was a low-budget movie shot in black and white with stylized sets. The simple filming style suited the rather serious subject matter and *Jailhouse Rock* is widely regarded as Elvis's best movie. *Jailhouse Rock* is most famous for an exciting dance sequence in which Elvis sings the title track, backed by professional dancers as inmates in a jail cellblock. Elvis had initially been unsure about the idea, but choreographer Alex Romero created a routine based on how the singer moved naturally on stage, so he felt comfortable and became more enthusiastic. Elvis got on well with professional dancer Russ Tamblyn, who coached him to develop his dancing style.

Above: Elvis performs on the set of *Jailhouse Rock* with Bill Black (bass), D. J. Fontana (drums), co-star Judy Tyler, songwriter Mike Stoller (piano) and Scotty Moore (guitar).

Drafted

Above: In 1957 Elvis received notification to attend a pre-induction physical to see if he was eligible for draft. The news that the famous ducktail and sideburns would soon be shorn off into a standard army short-back-and-sides made the front page of *Billboard*, and caused panic amongst the loyal fans. Elvis was based at Fort Hood, Texas, and Vernon and Gladys as well as Vernon's mother Minnie Presley soon followed him there. In August 1958 the hot Texas weather brought Gladys's health problems to a head. She returned to Memphis to see a doctor—and was rushed into hospital, where two days later she died. Elvis was inconsolable.

Opposite: Before entering the army Elvis gave one of his most critically acclaimed performances, as Danny Fisher in *King Creole*. Director Michael Curtiz had also been responsible for *Casablanca*; other film industry heavyweights on the production included Hall Wallis as producer and Russell Harlan as cinematographer. The expertise and experience lavished on the movie certainly showed on the screen.

After a while the other soldiers accepted him as "one of the boys" and, in some respects, this was one of the most "normal" periods of Elvis's entire life.

In 1959, Elvis was introduced to Priscilla Beaulieu, stepdaughter of an air force officer stationed in Germany.

Sergeant Presley

Shortly after his mother's death Elvis was transferred to a US base at Friedberg, near Frankfurt in Germany. There he was assigned to Company C, which had been chosen because it was the company that spent the most time away on manoeuvres— and thus away from public attention. Elvis drove a jeep for Reconnaissance Platoon Sergeant Ira Jones and, according to Jones, he "scrubbed, washed and greased" the jeep too. Elvis was promoted twice during his army career. In January 1960, just before his discharge, he rose to the rank of sergeant.

A return to Hollywood

In May 1960 Elvis began work on *G.I. Blues,* a musical comedy with a storyline that was heavily based on his army career. This was quickly followed up by *Flaming Star* and *Wild in the Country*—two movies with more serious themes.

In March 1961 Elvis began work on *Blue Hawaii.* It was the most successful movie commercially of his career. A light and amusing story, with more songs than ever before, the picture also made great use of the stunning Hawaiian scenery. The success of *Blue Hawaii* sealed Elvis's fate as far as his film career was concerned. Although *Flaming Star* and *Wild in the Country* had not lost money, neither had they done as well as Elvis movies were expected to. The Colonel used the amazing box-office success of *Blue Hawaii* to convince Elvis that his fans preferred him in lightweight musical comedies. Here he is pictured with his co-star, Joan Blackman.

The classic hits "Are You Lonesome Tonight?" and "It's Now or Never" both entered the Hot 100 in April 1960, remaining there for a total of 36 weeks.

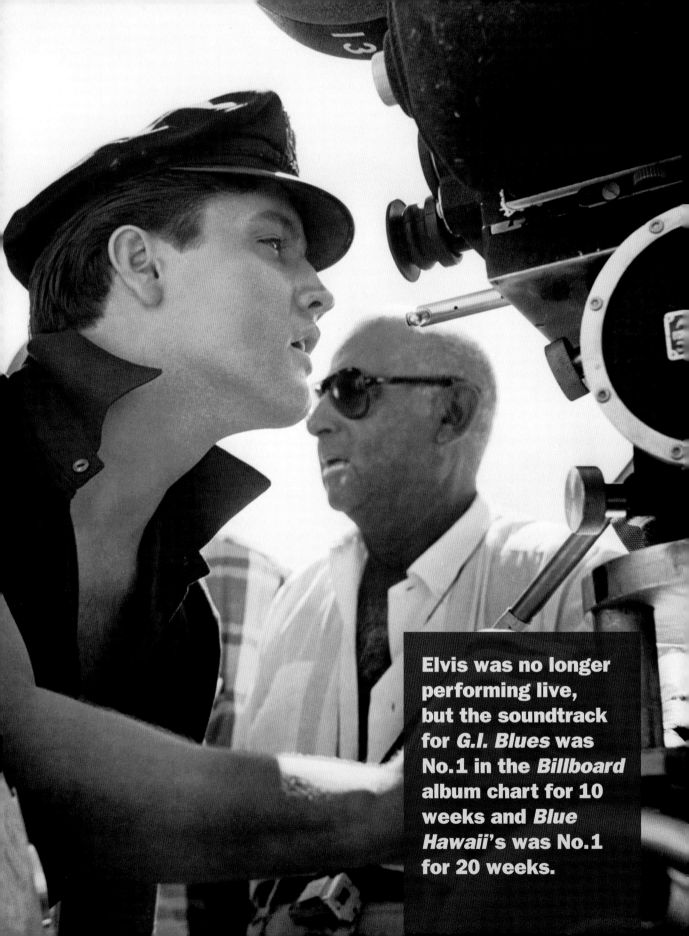

Elvis was no longer performing live, but the soundtrack for *G.I. Blues* was No.1 in the *Billboard* album chart for 10 weeks and *Blue Hawaii*'s was No.1 for 20 weeks.

Working with Ann-Margret

Right: In July of 1963 Elvis started work on his 15th movie, *Viva Las Vegas*. His co-star was Swedish actress and singer Ann-Margret and Elvis found that for once his partner could match his singing and dancing skills. In addition, the two stars quickly realized that they were kindred spirits, both full of energy and mischief.

Opposite: Elvis checks the view through the camera. Filming on *Fun in Acapulco* began in early 1963, after Elvis had spent Christmas with Priscilla at Graceland, the first time they had been together since he left Germany in 1960. Elvis had been trying to persuade her parents to let her come to America since then, and finally they had relented. After the success of Priscilla's visit, he persuaded her parents to allow her to finish her education in America.

Reluctant movie star

Above: Elvis and Joan O'Brien in *It Happened at the World's Fair*, which was made for MGM and filmed on location in Seattle. The wardrobe that was specially made for Elvis to wear in the movie cost $9,300 and included 10 suits, 30 shirts and 55 ties.

As Elvis focused increasingly on making movies record sales were falling: of all the singles released in 1965, only a gospel song, "Crying in the Chapel", made it into the *Billboard* Top 10, peaking at No. 3. The song had originally been recorded for *His Hand in Mine*, Elvis's first gospel LP, but was released as a single instead.

Opposite: A promotional portrait of Elvis dating from the mid-1960s. Elvis had now lost his initial enthusiasm for making movies, after realizing that he would never be respected as a serious actor.

In 1965 Elvis filmed *Harum Scarum, Frankie and Johnny* and *Paradise Hawaiian Style* while *Roustabout, Happy Girl* and *Tickle Me* were on release.

Right: Elvis in *Clambake* with Shelley Fabares. In the movie Elvis plays the son of a millionaire who agrees to trade places with a water skiing instructor, eager to see if he can be accepted for himself and not his money. The premise of the movie reflected Elvis's own situation since his fame and wealth isolated him from ordinary people.

Although Elvis now wanted to give up making movies, he still had contractual obligations, so the punishing production schedule continued. The Colonel was aware of Elvis's dissatisfaction and was attempting to find songs and scripts that Elvis liked but no one really wanted to tamper with what had previously been a winning formula.

Elvis had shocked many with his provocative performances at the start of his career, but in 1967 he won a Grammy for Best Sacred Performance with his recording of "How Great Thou Art".

Wedding bells

Right: Elvis and Priscilla are married in a private ceremony in a room at the Aladdin Hotel in Las Vegas on May 1, 1967, by the Nevada Supreme Court judge David Zenoff. Fourteen people were present at the ceremony, including Priscilla's parents and sister, Vernon and the Colonel. The newly-weds left for a month-long honeymoon at the Flying Circle G ranch in Wallis, Mississippi, a property Elvis had purchased in early 1967.

Getting married was not the only change Elvis wanted to make in his life. In 1968 he and Priscilla met Tom Jones after the Welsh singer's show at the Flamingo Hotel in Las Vegas. By that time Elvis had not sung in front of a live audience for several years, but he confided that he wanted to make a comeback—and that he would really like to perform in Las Vegas. The advent of The Beatles had ushered in a wave of popularity for groups and Elvis was concerned that perhaps solo singers were now seen as old-fashioned. However, seeing Tom Jones performing so successfully in Las Vegas convinced him otherwise.

Introducing Lisa Marie

Left: On February 1, 1968, exactly nine months after she and Elvis were married, Priscilla gave birth to a daughter weighing 6 lb 15 oz. Elvis was overjoyed at the idea of becoming a father. At a press conference he told journalists that he was the "happiest man in the world". Unfortunately, soon after Lisa Marie was born, Elvis made it clear to Priscilla that he was no longer physically attracted to her. Priscilla was left feeling unhappy and unfulfilled—and it would only be a matter of time before someone stepped in to comfort her.

Opposite: Nancy Sinatra with Elvis in *Speedway*. The two stars had been romantically linked before Elvis's marriage, but again rumours began to circulate. However, when Priscilla was expecting Lisa Marie, it was Nancy who organized the baby shower.

A change of habits

Left: Elvis and Colonel Parker on location during the filming of the last Presley movie, *Change of Habit*. By this time Elvis had decided that he wanted to return to singing and did not want to do any more films.

Charro!, Elvis's 29th movie, was released on March 13, 1969, just as filming for *Change of Habit* began in LA. *Charro!* was a new departure: an Elvis picture with no songs. The only time Elvis was heard singing was on the title song played over the credits. In this movie he appeared rugged and handsome in a beard, which certainly pleased the fans.

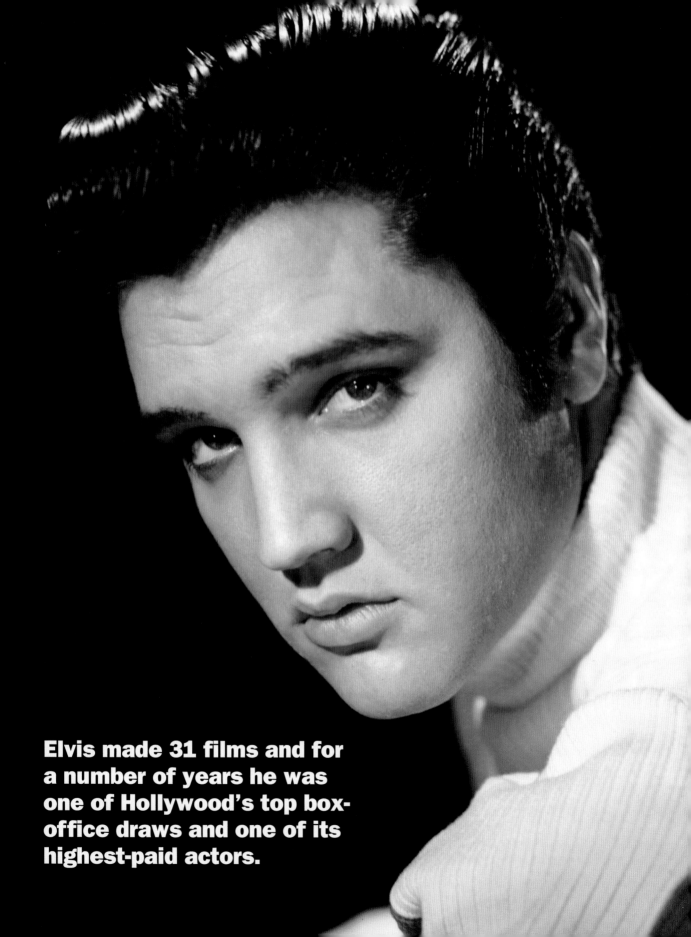

Elvis made 31 films and for a number of years he was one of Hollywood's top box-office draws and one of its highest-paid actors.

The '68 Comeback Special

By mid-1968 it had been decided that Elvis would appear in a Christmas special, to be broadcast on television by NBC. The programme was recorded before a live audience in June 1968—the first time that Elvis had appeared live for seven years. The original plan proposed by the Colonel was that Elvis would sing a selection of Christmas songs, but NBC wanted something a little more interesting and so director Steve Binder and his team decided to use the 60-minute slot to tell a story about a young man leaving home to search for happiness, the obstacles encountered along the way and the eventual journey back home. Elvis loved the whole idea and threw himself into the project with enthusiasm.

The *Special* was initially broadcast as a 60 minute programme but after Elvis died a longer version was released. Much of the unused *Special* footage was also packaged as *Elvis: One Night With You.*

A natural Instinct

Elvis initially seemed nervous at performing after such a long absence, and when he first walked out on to the stage he was shaky, but as the audience responded to him an amazing surge of confidence brought back his natural instinct for performing.

Opposite: For the finale, Elvis sang standing in front of his name in lights. The show was originally supposed to end with him singing a Christmas song, but—as they got to know Elvis better and saw how deeply he was affected by the deaths of Robert Kennedy and Martin Luther King—Steve Binder asked songwriter Earl Brown to write an inspirational song for the finale. That song was the much-loved "If I Can Dream" which was inspired by Martin Luther King's "I have a dream" speech. Elvis greatly admired King and had committed this speech to memory.

The *Special* aired on December 3, 1968, and was seen by 42 per cent of the viewing audience—giving NBC its biggest ratings victory of the year.

Comeback in Las Vegas

Above: After the '68 Comeback Special was transmitted fans both old and new rushed to buy his records, and Elvis announced that he wanted to return to singing. The Colonel organized a four-week booking at the International Hotel in Las Vegas, which was due to open in July 1969. The show was a sensational success, and the hotel booked him to appear twice a year for the next five years. Here Elvis and Vernon chat at a press conference following the first night of his Las Vegas show. His performance had finished with four standing ovations, and critics called it "a mesmerizing performance".

"I'm really glad to be back in front of a live audience. I don't think I have ever been more excited than I was tonight."

That's The Way It Is

Below: A still from *That's The Way It Is*, a 1970 documentary showing Elvis on tour. The filmmakers Bob Abel and Pierre Adidge had the most up-to-date mobile cameras and other state-of-the-art equipment, and they followed Elvis around for some time, recording him as if he were a mythical hero on a quest. As well as recording performances, they showed life backstage, candid footage and highlights from the past. The resulting film was a refreshing record of Elvis at his peak, full of spontaneity and movement. The two filmmakers had even won over Colonel Parker, who said, "Go out there and make the best film ever". And that is pretty much what they did— even today, the documentary is one of the classic records of a star on tour.

> **"A live concert to me is exciting because of all the electricity that is generated in the crowd and on stage. It's my favourite part of the business."**

Aloha from Hawaii

Left: Elvis appeared at Madison Square Garden in New York for the first time in 1972. There were four concerts, which were followed by a short tour. The concerts were a great success—all four performances were sold out.

Opposite: In January 1973 the Colonel came up with a project which was not only massive in scale but also innovative in concept. Elvis had been wanting to do a worldwide tour for some time, but this had never come off. Instead the Colonel arranged the next best thing—a television special in Hawaii that would be beamed live by satellite to countries all over the world. Elvis looked slim, fit and handsome in Hawaii but throughout 1973 the combination of the breakdown of his marriage and a punishing tour and recording schedule, with very little rest, adversely affected his already poor health.

Aloha from Hawaii was seen in more American households than man's first walk on the moon, and in around 40 countries by nearly 1.5 billion people.

The King is dead

Elvis had turned 40 in January 1975 and at the end of the month he was rushed to hospital with severe stomach pains. A week later Vernon had a heart attack and joined him in the same hospital. After they were both discharged, Elvis went back to Graceland to try to rest, lose more weight and get his medication under control, but his good resolutions did not last.

On June 26, 1977, Elvis appeared in a concert at the Market Square Arena in Indianapolis—it would be his very last concert performance. He returned to Graceland to rest before the tour resumed but on August 16 there was a worldwide outpouring of grief when it was announced that Elvis had died.

This is a Transatlantic Press book
First published in 2012

Transatlantic Press
38 Copthorne Road
Croxley Green, Hertfordshire
WD3 4AQ, UK

Text © Transatlantic Press
All images © Getty Images

A catalogue record for this book is available from the British Library.

ISBN: 978-1-908533-97-5

Printed in China